The Berenstain Bears®
LOST IN A CAVE

Stan & Jan Berenstain

Reader's Digest Kids

Westport, Connecticut

Today was the day the Bear Scouts were going to try to win their Spooky Cave Merit Badges.

Scout Sister looked up at Spooky Cave. "I'm scared," she said.

"Me too," said Scout Brother.

"That makes three of us," said Scout Fred.

"Nonsense!" said Scoutmaster Papa.
"I know all about caves. And I know
Spooky Cave is nothing to be afraid of.

"Come! If you want to win your Spooky
Cave Merit Badges, follow me!"

But Spooky Cave did look a
little scary. It looked like a big
mouth with sharp teeth. And the
rocks around it made it look like a
big monster face.

The mountain goats
watched as Papa and the
scouts went into Spooky
Cave.

"It looks strange in here," said Scout Brother.

"What are those pointy things?" asked Scout Sister.

"I know all about caves," said Scoutmaster Papa. "So I'm glad you asked me that question. They are sta-lac-tites and sta-lag-mites." They were hard words, so Papa said them very slowly.

"Which are which?"
asked Scout Fred.

"Here's a little rhyme to help
you remember," said Papa.

"Stalactites and stalagmites,
only caves have got 'em.
Tites are always on the top,
and mites are on the bottom."

The scouts looked up. The stalactites
looked very sharp. What if one should fall?

"It sounds strange in here,"
said Scout Sister. "Why is that?"

"I know all about caves," said
Papa. "So I'm glad you asked me
that question. It sounds strange
because of the echo. Listen." Then
he shouted, "*HELLO!*"

"HELLO! Hello! Hello!"
came the echo as the sound
of Papa's voice bounced
between the walls of the cave.

But there was something Papa did not know. He did not know you shouldn't make loud noises in a cave. Loud noises can shake things loose.

"Look out!" said the scouts.

A big stalactite was falling—
and it was pointing straight
at *Papa's* bottom.

"Yipe!" said Papa as
he jumped out of the way.

Papa and the scouts went
deeper and deeper into the cave.

After a while, the scouts could
not remember which way they
had come.

"Papa," said Sister. "Are we lost?"

"I know all about caves," said
Papa. "So I'm glad you asked me
that question." He held up a ball of
string. "We can't get lost because I
left a trail of string."

But there was something else
Papa did not know. He did not
know that a mountain goat had
followed them. The mountain
goat had eaten the trail of
string.

"What shall we do? What shall
we do?" asked the scouts.

"Another good question," said
Papa. Then he put his finger in his
mouth and held it up in the air.
"Aha!" he said. "I feel a breeze. That
means there's another way out.

"Follow me!"

But there was one more thing
Papa did not know. He did not
know about the underground
stream. "Yiiiee!" shouted Papa.
"Help!" shouted the scouts.

Down,
down,
they went.

Down,
down,
down

and out
of Spooky Cave.

They were
at the bottom
of the mountain.

"Here are your Spooky Cave
Merit Badges," said Papa.

"That was fun," said Scout
Sister.

"Yes," said Scout Brother.
"It was just like the big water ride
at Fun Park!"

"May we do it again?" asked Scout Fred.

"I know all about caves," said Papa.

"So I'm glad you asked me that question.

The answer is a big, loud...

But the scouts didn't mind. They were proud of their Spooky Cave Merit Badges. And they were proud of Scoutmaster Papa, who knew everything there was to know about caves.

Well…

almost everything.